THE CHRISTMAS DOG

(Originally published as THE DECEMBER DOG)

Jan M. Robinson

Text illustrated by Joan Sandin

Weekly Reader Books
Middletown, Connecticut

To my mother, Janice Howes Lenoue

Copyright © 1969 by Jan M. Robinson
All rights reserved. Printed in U.S.A.

Weekly Reader Books Edition published by
arrangement with J. D. Lippincott Company

THE CHRISTMAS DOG

I

THE last drops of May rain dried on the new leaves, and steam wisped up from the humus carpet in the woods. A clump of fiddlehead ferns uncurled in the sun nearly hiding the figure behind it. The red dog stood poised, a front foot raised, as she gazed out into the clearing.

The warm spring rain had soaked the new growth and filled it with life. Red trillium and pale yellow adder's-tongue bloomed brightly through their mulch of leaves, and overhead, white shad blossoms dappled the hazy sky.

The dog crouched until her belly nearly brushed the ground and crept forward toward a chipmunk that was digging around a rotten stump. The chipmunk scurried about, exploring little caves in the pulpy wood. Sometimes, he found a seed and paused to eat it while his whiskers quivered and his beady eyes darted about the clearing.

The dog inched toward him. She was a small dog with thick red fur that bronzed at the tips. Her ears were pointed and erect over a small face and delicate black muzzle. Pressed against the ground with only her sides moving, she looked like a fox.

The chipmunk left the stump and scampered across the clearing. With two graceful leaps the dog caught him and trotted back to the ferns. She tossed the tiny animal down with a gulp and packed down a spot under the ferns to lie down. She lay with her muzzle stretched across her front paws and gazed into the clearing, her eyes slitted against the glare of the sun.

The dog had once belonged to a junkman named Jake Higgins. Jake lived on the outskirts of Ashley and collected wrecked cars and scrap metal. He lived alone in a shack at the edge of his mountainous pile of rubble.

Someone had given Jake the dog as a puppy because Jake had talked about getting a dog to guard his junk yard when he was away collecting scrap. Sometimes boys came and took parts off Jake's old cars so he had wanted a watchdog to frighten them away.

He had named the puppy Kit because she looked like a baby fox.

Jake had tied the puppy to the dilapidated porch with a greasy rope and every time he walked up or down the porch steps, Jake kicked at the puppy. He didn't intend to be mean, he just considered it part of the dog's training. He thought a watchdog had to be vicious. At night, when he fed her, he was almost kind. He even talked to her but the rest of the time he was surly and the dog was afraid of him.

Whenever anyone came to the junk yard, Kit would run out to the end of her rope and wag her tail. She didn't want to be a watchdog, she wanted to play and be friendly.

People began to laugh at Jake and tease him about his "ferocious" watchdog. This made Jake very angry and after any visitors had left, he would have an extra kick or two for Kit.

One day when Jake kicked at the dog, she dodged his heavy boot and he kicked the rope instead. The rotten fibers parted. Jake was thrown off balance and tumbled onto the driveway as Kit stumbled backward onto her haunches. For a moment they sat facing each other, then Kit rose and trotted off toward the woods.

The little dog traveled through the woods to the other side of Ashley and spent a raw winter on her own. She had been hungry and lonely but nothing could draw her back to the junk yard and Jake. She had grown gaunt as she waited for spring. Now the sun warmed her and her belly was full and, under the ferns, she slept the light sleep of wild things.

2

A warm breeze played through the clearing and stirred the fiddleheads where the dog lay. She wiggled her nose in her sleep for a moment before she raised her head and sniffed the air. The musty tang of the damp ground filled her nostrils and she stretched lazily as a chickadee looked down from a nearby pine and scolded loudly. Kit rose and trotted across the clearing toward the brook.

Kit loved the brook. She walked through a patch of rubbery skunk cabbage and slid into the cool clear water. She waded in belly deep and watched small trout and minnows darting about her legs. She waited until one of the fish swam near the surface, then she dipped her muzzle in the water and snapped. All she came up with was a snout full of water. She sneezed and continued to watch and snap at the fish until at last she tired of the game.

Kit climbed the bank on the other side of the brook and shook herself dry. The brook separated the woods from the meadow. Beyond the meadow, there was a farm. The dog liked to cross the meadow and watch the Martins' farm on the other side. She would hide in the tall grass and listen to the human voices and barn sounds and thump her tail contentedly. She was afraid to venture beyond the grass but she was continually drawn to the Martins whose voices she heard from her blind of timothy and clover.

As she watched from her hiding place, she came to know the farm family. There was a man, a woman, a little girl, and a boy named Lon. Kit knew the boy's name because she had heard it called so often.

Kit watched through the grass as Lon slipped around behind the milk house with a fish pole over his shoulder.

"Lon!"

The boy stopped and looked down at the gravel path. "What, Mom?"

"Have you finished your chores?" his mother called from the kitchen door.

Lon picked up a stone with his toe and tossed it against the milk house. "Not yet but gee, I haven't been fishing for a week."

It was a moment before his mother answered. "All right this time but be sure you get home in time to finish them before dinner."

The boy grinned and trotted toward the meadow almost forgetting to call back "Thanks" to his mother. Kit flattened herself to the ground. Lon was heading right toward her. If she ran, the boy would see her.

Lon slowed to a walk when he came to the meadow and parted the grass a few feet down from the dog. Kit hugged the ground as she felt the boy's scent tingle in her nostrils. She tried not to move but she couldn't control the tip of her tail which was wagging ever so slightly.

Lon was watching for woodchucks so when he saw the grass ripple, he stopped. He watched the place where he had seen the

faint movement but nothing more happened. He took a step toward the spot and nearly tripped on the dog before he noticed her. For an instant, the boy's blue eyes met the brown-yellow eyes of the dog. Then she bounded away and was swallowed up in the sea of meadow grass.

Kit streaked across the field until she reached the brook. She leaped the narrow banks and slipped into the woods. She ran but not from fear. There was something playful in the way she ran. Her leaps were high and bounding and her tail swept in circles behind her.

In the woods, Kit slowed to a trot and headed toward the overhanging rock where she slept. She crawled under the rock where the dirt was cool and looked out at the woods, her head resting on her front paws. Far away a woodpecker drummed on a rotten tree and, overhead, two jays quarreled noisily.

Kit's tail thumped on the dirt floor of her cave and she wanted to go back to the boy but she couldn't move. Her year in the woods had made her too shy and wary for a close human encounter.

3

IT was a week before Kit started watching the Martin farm again and now she proceeded more cautiously. One day on her way back from watching, she met a small pack of dogs at the brook. This was a particularly unruly pack that had been running deer and killing chickens all over Ashley. Sometimes Kit had found their scent in the woods but this was the first time she had seen them.

There were just three dogs in the pack. A beagle, a yellow mongrel, and a big silver German shepherd. The three dogs were males. The hair along their backs bristled as the two larger dogs voiced throaty growls. Kit felt the hair along her back rise and she curled her lip in a toothy snarl. The shepherd left the pack and approached her stiff-legged.

Kit tucked her tail between her hind legs and faced him. The dog circled several times before he came close enough to sniff her nose. When the shepherd was through, he allowed the other dogs to come and sniff noses with her, too.

Then, the introductions over, the dogs tried to urge Kit to follow them. She trailed them reluctantly through the woods with the beagle snapping playfully at her heels until they reached the road into Ashley. The woods ended abruptly on top of a high ledge that overlooked the road. Kit stopped on top of the ledge and watched the dogs slide down in a shower of gravel and stones to the highway below. The shepherd returned and tried to coax Kit to follow them but she wouldn't go beyond the confines of her own territory.

Kit sat on the ledge and watched the dogs disappear down the highway. It was dusk and

she watched the sun streak the sky with ribbons of pink and lavender. Far down the road, she heard the beagle baying and read his message of a rabbit chase. But Kit did not respond. She was a silent hunter.

She caught a field mouse on her way back through the woods. Usually after a late meal she was ready to retire to her rock under the hemlocks but tonight she was restless. She had visited the farm after a week's absence

and listened to the Martins' voices. She had run for a while with the dog pack and enjoyed their companionship. Through the night, the little dog roamed the woods. She traveled as far north as the old stone quarry and south to the highway. She heard owls hooting through the night, and toward dawn she heard whippoorwills calling by the brook.

The hazy yellow morning found her trotting toward the brook as if in answer to the whippoorwills' call. She trotted wearily up the bank and stopped. Lon was fishing on the other side.

The boy sat with his fish pole across his knees, making chains out of dandelion stems. He saw the dog but he didn't move. The breeze was blowing toward Lon so Kit didn't catch his scent until she had made her blunder. The dog had crouched down and was creeping backward down the bank when Lon spoke. "You're really getting careless, Little Fox. That's twice now."

Kit disappeared over the bank but Lon knew she was still listening so he continued to talk. "What's the matter? You surprised I knew about you? Why, I've been watching you almost since you've been watching me. I've been watching you and wondering what happened to you before you came to the woods to live. Are you still listening, Little Fox?"

Kit crept down the mossy bank until she felt the woods at her back. She waited for a moment under the branches of a low poplar, listening, then she turned and trotted into the woods until the voice was just a whisper behind her.

4

KIT changed her watering place to a spot farther down the brook. Here, the stream widened and the banks flattened out even with the meadow, and the water was shallow and gurgled over the gravelly bottom. Since her last encounter with Lon, Kit had stopped visiting the Martin farm.

One day in the late summer when Kit was cooling off in the brook, the dog pack trotted out of the woods and joined her in the water. She recognized the three dogs she had seen before but two new dogs had joined the pack. There was a huge black hound and a husky. The hound acknowledged her with a friendly wag of his tail but the husky stood with his front paws in the water growling. He was a heavy dog with a wide forehead and slanted eyes. His lips twisted in a savage grin as he stepped into the water and advanced toward Kit.

Kit snarled and backed out of the water across the flat mudbank until she stopped abruptly under the roots of an overturned poplar. She crouched there trapped as the husky churned through the shallow water toward her.

On the opposite bank, the shepherd roared

a challenge and leaped into the water. The husky turned but not fast enough to dodge the blow from the shepherd's shoulder as he plowed past. The two dogs fought in the water, growling and sputtering until the stream was muddy and froth edged the banks.

The other dogs watched calmly while the two dogs battled their way back and forth across the brook. Finally the shepherd got a grip on the husky's neck and tossed him up on the bank. The husky lay on his side, his lips curled up over his teeth, waiting for the shepherd to strike. The shepherd stood over him for a moment, then he turned and crossed the brook to where Kit was huddled under the poplar roots.

Kit followed the shepherd back to the other dogs and they headed into the woods. The husky was sullen and strayed off to one side casting vicious glances at the shepherd.

They treed a porcupine and chased squirrels. Kit, who was only accustomed to hunting to survive, wondered at the dogs' foolish sport.

At dusk, they went back to the brook. The shepherd, who was leading, stopped and sniffed the breeze. A deer was drinking at the brook. The doe lifted her muzzle and a thin stream of water trickled into the ripples her nose had made. Her ears flapped to keep the cloud of mosquitoes away from her head.

She stood for a moment gazing at the thicket where the dogs hid, then a twig snapped and she leaped out of the water. The dogs lunged out of the brush and splashed across the brook behind her.

The black hound and the beagle bayed as they felt the thrill of the chase but the other dogs ran silently. They raced through the woods until they came to the ledge over the highway. The deer bounded up the stone slabs and paused a second on top before she leaped down the rocky incline and crossed the road to the thick pines on the other side.

Kit followed the dogs to the top of the ledge and stopped. This was the end of her territory. She slipped off to the side and watched them scramble their way down the rocks to the highway. They reached the road and had just started across when a rifle cracked somewhere in the dim light. The yellow mongrel fell in the road as the other dogs raced to reach the other side. The rifle cracked again and the black hound spun around in the highway and collapsed in the ditch on the other side.

Kit flattened herself to the ground at the top of the ledge, too frightened to move. A car pulled up from down the road and stopped beside the yellow dog. Two men got

out of the car. One man was the game warden. The other was Mr. Martin. They opened the trunk of the car and tossed the two dogs in. The game warden squinted toward the pines where the pack had disappeared. "I'm going to get those dogs if it's the last thing I do. Especially that shepherd. He's the leader. They've pulled down three deer this summer and it'll be worse this winter. The deer count's low enough as it is. Any idea who that shepherd belongs to?"

Mr. Martin shook his head. "No, but he's certainly a beautiful dog. Must belong to someone. I've never seen him before. In fact, I've never seen any of these dogs. If you hadn't asked me to help you tonight, I probably wouldn't even have known about them. The only dog I've heard of lately is the one Lon calls Little Fox. Glad to see she wasn't running with the pack."

The warden closed the trunk and emptied his gun. "What's this Little Fox, a stray dog? They're nothing but trouble. Half that pack are probably strays."

Mr. Martin clicked an empty shell out of the chamber of his rifle. "Lon says she's a wild dog. He's been watching her for quite a while but he can't get near her. Someone must have really hurt her once."

The game warden pulled the keys out of the trunk and started for the car door. "Someone probably did. That's the problem with these dogs, most of them anyway. People want them but then they don't take care of them. Well, I hope for Lon's sake she doesn't start running deer with these dogs. 'Cause if she does, there'll be a bullet for her, too."

5

SUMMER lazed through the month of September and on into the middle of October before the first frost came. During the night, the temperature dropped and Kit woke to a forest of frost that sparkled in the sun and shimmered on the red and yellow maple leaves.

The leaves crunched under her feet as she trotted to the brook and the woods was filled with fall excitement. Blue jays screamed through the branches and squirrels and chipmunks rummaged about under the leaves for seeds and acorns for winter storage.

Kit approached the brook and was surprised to see the German shepherd standing in the water. She hadn't seen any of the dogs since the deer chase. She stopped and wagged her tail happily.

The two dogs romped through the woods. They explored the stone quarry and teased the porcupines that lived there. They rolled in hemlock needles and chased through the leaves that carpeted the ground.

The shepherd stayed for three days, then he left the woods. Kit followed him to the ledge over the highway but the big dog couldn't coax her to go any farther. Kit left him and swung back into the woods.

Now Kit was caught up in the bustle of approaching winter. She dug more dirt out from under the rock and made the hole deeper. She kicked dry leaves in to cover the floor. She hunted more diligently for she recalled the hunger of the past winter. Her coat grew thick as she watched the other animals prepare for winter and disappear, and the nights grew quiet and long.

One day on her rounds through the woods, she heard the Martin children. Kit ducked under some low hemlocks and waited. Soon they burst through the underbrush. They were carrying baskets to fill with acorns and butternuts. Lon strode ahead while his sister struggled to keep up. "Hey, slow down! Your legs are longer than mine."

Lon laughed. "Okay, Shorty, there's no hurry anyway." He slowed his pace and Beth caught up to him.

It was cold in the woods and steam plumed from their mouths. They neared the oak trees and Beth stopped. "While you're getting acorns, can I go over to the old apple tree and get some bittersweet for Mom?"

Lon balanced his basket on his head and thought a minute. "Okay, but don't go anywhere else. I want to be able to find you when it's time to leave."

The children separated and Kit, who had been watching, came to the place where they parted and sniffed the ground. She was drawn to the more familiar scent of the boy but something about the small girl fascinated her and she turned to the left, the way Beth had taken.

Beth found the apple tree in a small clearing and looked up through twisted branches to the ropes of bright bittersweet that wound themselves up through the top limbs. She set her basket on the ground and swung up into the lower branches. It was an easy tree to climb and soon Beth was sitting among the gay clusters of orange berries at the top. She gathered a big bunch of bittersweet and started down the tree.

Kit watched from the cover of a juniper bush. Suddenly a limb popped loudly in the clear air and Beth tumbled out of the tree. It was a short fall but Beth, who didn't want to damage the bittersweet, made no attempt to catch herself. She landed on her back with the berries clutched in her hands and bumped her head against the trunk of the tree. Kit waited but the little girl didn't move.

As Kit watched, a strange instinct stirred in

her and she forgot her fear. She trotted across the clearing and sniffed the girl's face. There was no response so Kit nudged her with her nose. Slowly, the little girl's eyes blinked open and she gazed up into the pointed red face of the dog. For a moment neither of them moved, then Kit slipped away and disappeared into the woods.

Beth sat up and stared after the dog as Lon stepped into the clearing. "What did you do, fall out of the tree? I knew I shouldn't have let you come here alone."

Beth stood up and leaned against the trunk of the tree. "I saw her, Lon! I saw Little Fox! I fell and bumped my head and she came to see if I was all right. I think I was knocked out 'cause when I opened my eyes, she was looking at me. You're right, she does look like a fox. A beautiful red fox!"

Lon looked at his little sister. He was sorry

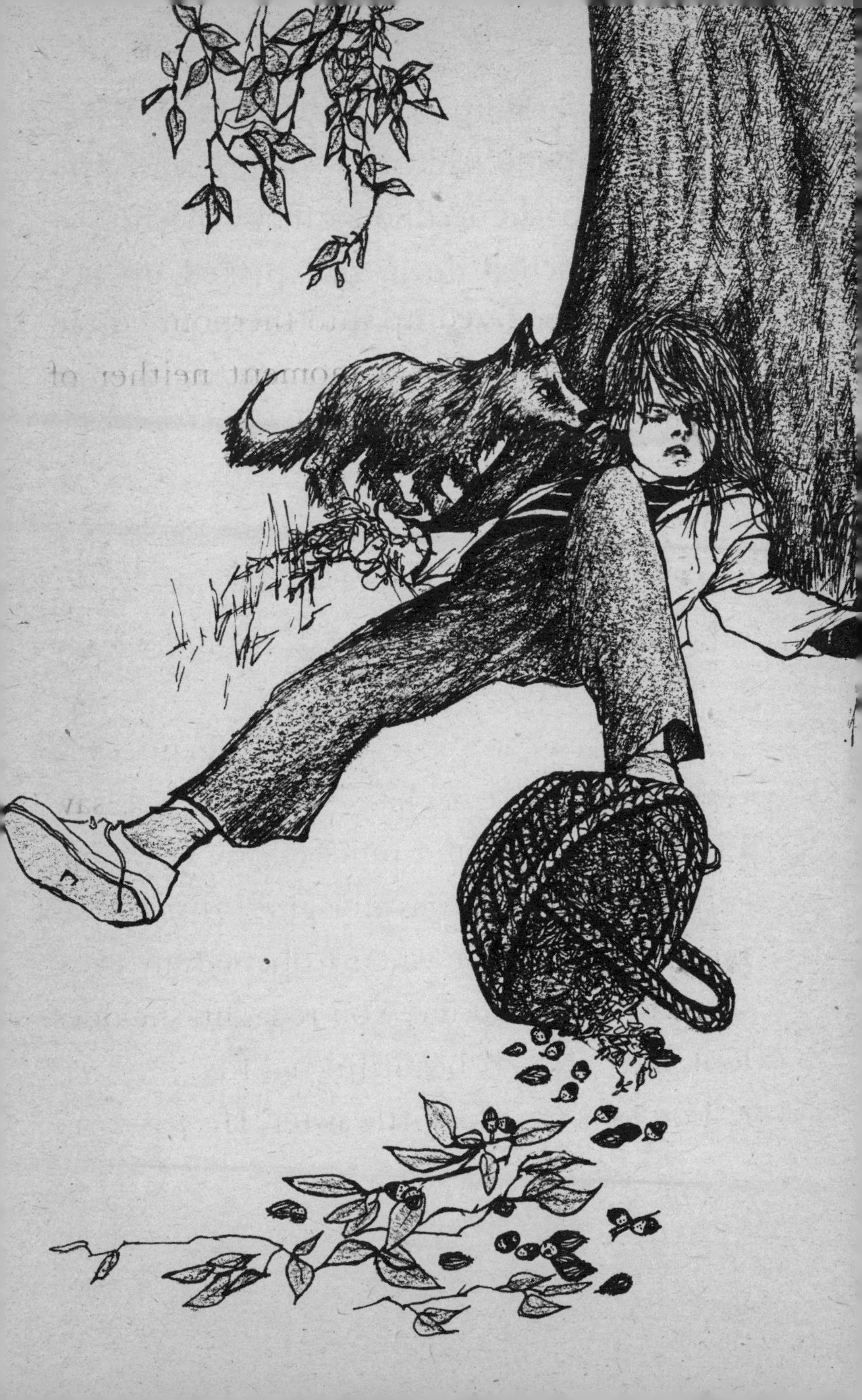

she had fallen but he couldn't help but feel jealous that she had been so close to Little Fox after he had tried so hard to befriend the dog. He reached down and picked up her basket. "Come on, let's go home and show Mom the bittersweet you nearly broke your neck getting."

6

FALL passed in a busy hustle until the trees were bare and the small animals who had been storing food holed up for the winter. The forest was quiet and a bitter cold settled over the countryside. One night early in December, the first snow fell. It sifted down through the hemlocks and covered the needles outside Kit's den.

At dawn, when the dog woke, the ground was covered with a layer of soft, new snow. Kit left the canopy of hemlock and blinked at the bright whiteness. She started for the stone quarry in search of food. She moved slowly for she was heavy with the litter that would soon be born.

Kit caught a pheasant near the quarry and hurried with it through the woods. The scent of bobcat was all around the place and she was instinctively afraid of this animal although she had never seen it. She ate the pheasant in a clearing and made the rounds of her territory.

After the night of the first snowfall, a cruel winter settled upon the land. The wind roared down from the north, stopping just long enough for more snow to fall, then it resumed its bitter howling. Branches cracked and snapped in the cold and game became scarce as small animals and birds remained in their protected places.

Kit roamed the woods in search of food. One day, she came upon the children cutting a balsam in the swampy part of the woods. She ducked under cover and listened. Lon had chosen a thick, bushy tree and was hacking at the trunk with his hatchet. "This is the one I wanted last year but it was too small then. Look at how much it has grown!"

Beth clapped her mittened hands together to keep them warm. "Everything grew this year. Dad says it was that kind of a summer." She stamped her feet in the snow and felt her toes tingle. "I wonder how the animals stand it when it gets this cold. I wonder what Little Fox does in this kind of weather. Do you think we'll see her, Lon?"

Lon stopped chopping and looked into the woods thoughtfully. "I haven't seen a sign of her in ages. I looked all through the woods on our way here but I didn't even see a track. I think she's gone."

"Could be," Beth agreed. "I wonder if Little Fox is here, what she eats when the animals all hibernate. She must be hungry. I looked for tracks, too, but the way the wind is blowing, they would be covered right up anyway."

Lon picked up his hatchet and gave the

tree a final chop. It toppled over in the snow with a soft swishing sound. "Boy, this will make a great Christmas tree! It's a fat one, the kind Mom likes. Do you want to drag first or shall I?"

Beth took the butt of the tree and started pulling. "You chopped it down so I'll drag first. Let's go, my feet are frozen."

When the children were out of sight, Kit rose and trotted back to the overhanging rock. She crawled under the shelter and nosed around. Some snow had blown under the rock during her absence. She began to dig. A shower of dirt and snow flew out of the opening under the rock. She made her bed deeper and rooted the floor with her nose to pack it down. She pulled dry leaves from a crevice and lined the floor of her cave. Finally, satisfied with her efforts, she curled up and fell asleep.

During the night, the wind howled outside and shrieked through the hemlock branches but Kit lay snugly under the rock and gave birth to her litter. The first two puppies were small reddish-brown females. Kit licked them dry and waited for the next one to be born. The third and last puppy was different from the other two. He was much larger with a wide forehead and heavy, square shoulders. He was a strange brindled mixture of the shepherd's silver coat and Kit's red hair. As he lay with his two dainty sisters and his little mother, he looked like a wolf cub and very much out of place. Kit cleaned all the puppies again and fell asleep with them nursing comfortably beside her.

7

IT was the day before Christmas and the puppies were nine days old. Their eye slits were starting to open and they were already roughhousing in the dim light of the cave. They were round and fat but Kit was having a difficult time finding food. The snow was deep, the wind still howled from the north and game was scarce. Her hunting trips took her farther and farther away from the rock and she was growing lean.

Kit stood up in the pocket under the rock and walked stiffly to the entrance. The puppies whimpered and she nudged them gently before she stepped outside into the cold. The wind had died down and the sun glared off the icy whiteness. It looked like a good day for hunting. Kit trotted through the snow to the brook. On good days the rabbits came there to nibble willow shoots.

Kit packed down a place in the snow under a laurel and lay down to wait. Soon two rabbits hopped into the willows and began to feed. The rabbits were white with a few dark hairs in their coats. Kit watched as they fed closer to where she was hiding. Soon they were very near the laurel and Kit shifted her weight to her hindquarters to spring. The largest rabbit stopped nibbling and wiggled his nose in the direction of the bush. His ears were rigid as he raised slightly on his hind legs, then he thumped the ground with his back feet and leaped away in a shower of snow. At the same instant, Kit sprang upon the smaller rabbit and caught it in mid-air by the back of the neck.

8

KIT carried the rabbit back to the laurel and fed leisurely. It was her first food in two days and the sun felt warm on her back. When the rabbit was gone, she gulped a mouthful of snow and trotted back to the rock.

As the dog approached her shelter, the hair

along the back of her neck bristled and she stopped and growled low in her throat. She could smell the gamey scent of the bobcat still heavy in the air. She put her nose to the snow and followed his spoor to the opening under the rock. She stopped in the entrance and whined but there was no answering sound from inside. She hurried under the rock and nosed around the empty cave. It reeked of bobcat. She backed out and sniffed the snow outside the den.

Kit found a small bloodstain in the snow and nosed it for a long time. Finally, she sat in the snow outside the cave, threw her head back and howled a long wail that penetrated the farthest part of the forest. The birds stopped their chatter and only the echo of Kit's cry hung in the frosty air.

The woods were silent and a soft snow began to fall as Kit slipped under the rock and packed down her bed. She curled up with her muzzle stretched across her front paws and looked out at the falling snow. Suddenly, she lifted her head and pricked her ears forward. A tiny sound came to her in the stillness.

Kit hurried outside and listened. The noise came again. She followed the sound and nosed around in the snow. Nearly hidden under a juniper and covered with snow, was the male puppy. He was quite a distance from the rock. The bobcat must have dropped him at the sound of Kit's approach.

Kit lifted the puppy and carried him back to the cave. He shivered and she scrubbed him warm with her tongue. His foreleg was hurt and he whimpered as he nursed beside her. Finally, with his belly full of warm milk and his mother to comfort him, the puppy

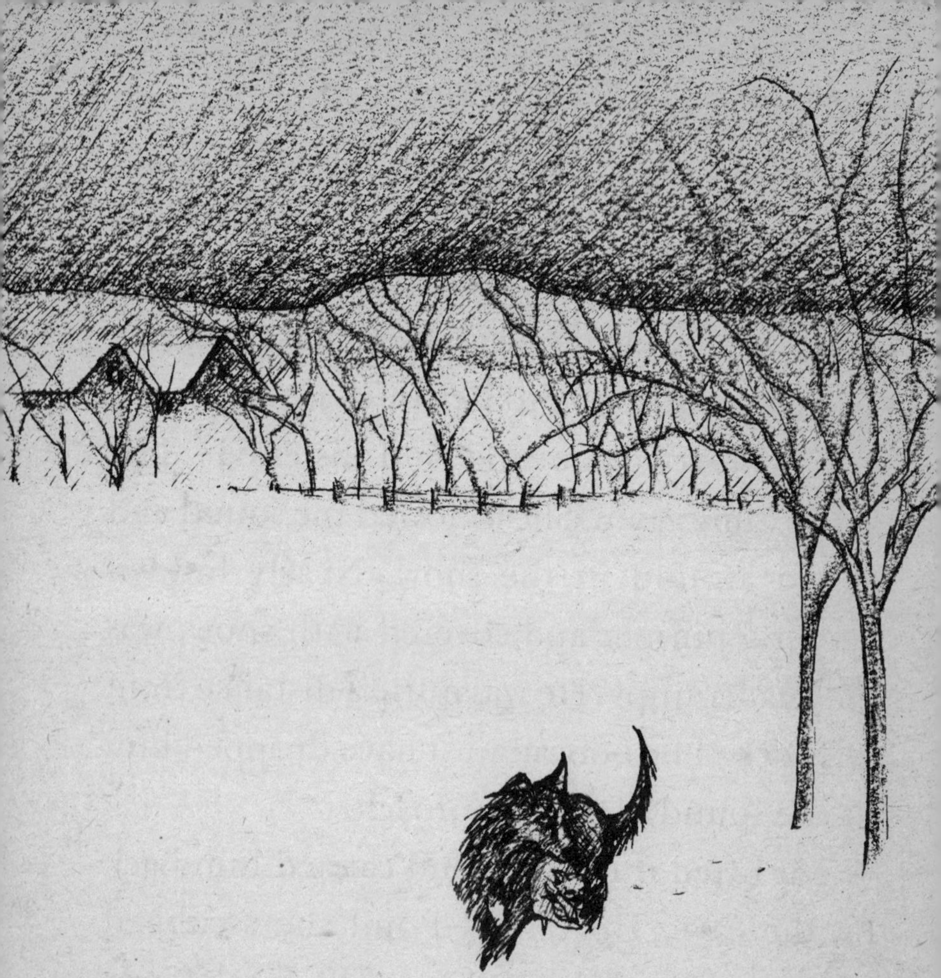

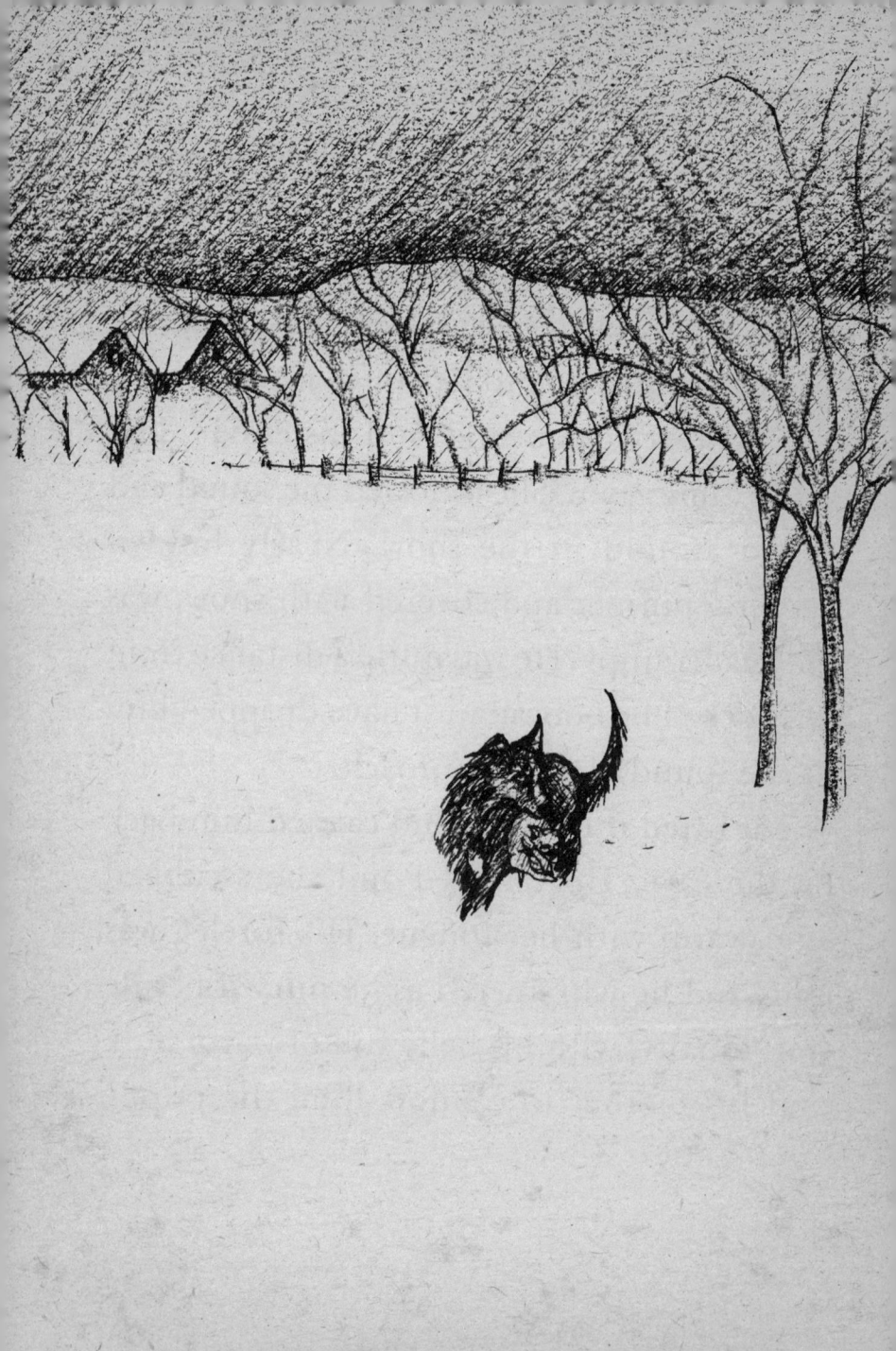

fell asleep. Sometimes in his sleep he would cry out and Kit would nudge him and snuggle closer.

While the puppy slept, Kit listened to the wind howl outside, and fear and loneliness crept over her. If she left the rock for food, the bobcat might return. The puppy was hurt and her licking didn't stop his pain. Food was scarce and winter was only beginning. She rose slowly and the puppy whimpered. Then, very gently, she lifted the puppy in her mouth and stepped out into the cold winter night.

Kit carried the puppy across the frozen brook and crossed the meadow. She saw lights in the Martin house. The barn was lighted, too. She stopped at the edge of the meadow and watched as Lon crossed the yard with a pail of milk in each hand and entered the house. She could smell the milk and her mouth watered.

The barn lights went out and Mr. Martin crossed the yard carrying more pails of milk. Kit moved closer to the house. A shower of colored lights reflected off the snow from the Christmas tree in the living-room window. A cow mooed softly in the barn as Kit crossed the yard to the back steps. The puppy hung limp in her mouth.

Kit's neck and jaw ached from the weight of the puppy. She set him in the snow at the bottom of the steps and nudged him. The puppy tucked his feet tight up under him and whined. Inside the house, Kit could hear the Martins laughing and talking. She could smell food and feel the warmth of the kitchen. She barked one timid, sharp bark and backed off several paces.

In a moment, the kitchen door opened and

Lon squinted out in the moonlight. Kit had picked up the puppy and stood with it dangling from her mouth. Lon wanted to rush out to her but he didn't dare move. Any quick movement might frighten her away. Instead, he began to talk. "Hey, Little Fox, did you smell the turkey cooking? Did you smell all that good stuff and decide to bring the family for Christmas dinner?" Then in a softer voice for his eyes were accustomed to the light and he could see how thin Kit was and how weak the puppy seemed, "Or do you need help? Poor little dog. Come on, Little Fox. No one's going to hurt you."

Beth heard Lon's voice and stood beside him as he whispered, "You stay here. I'm going to try to help Little Fox." He stepped outside and shivered in the cold. It was too late to go back for a jacket, the dog might leave. He started down the steps and Kit moved back. Lon inched forward, talking all the time. "I can't help you if you back all the way to the brook. Stand still, girl, that's a good dog."

He reached the dog and put the back of his hand to her nose. Kit sniffed warily then he let it slide up her nose to her ears which he rubbed gently. As he stroked her with his right hand, he slipped his left hand under the puppy and supported its weight. In a moment, Kit released her hold on the puppy and it dropped into Lon's hand. Lon looked back at Beth and called softly, "I've got the puppy, what do I do now?"

"I don't know. Keep patting Little Fox and I'll ask Dad."

She disappeared and Lon continued to stroke the dog. She was smaller than he had thought. Most of her was long red hair. Soon Mr. Martin appeared at the door. Lon looked

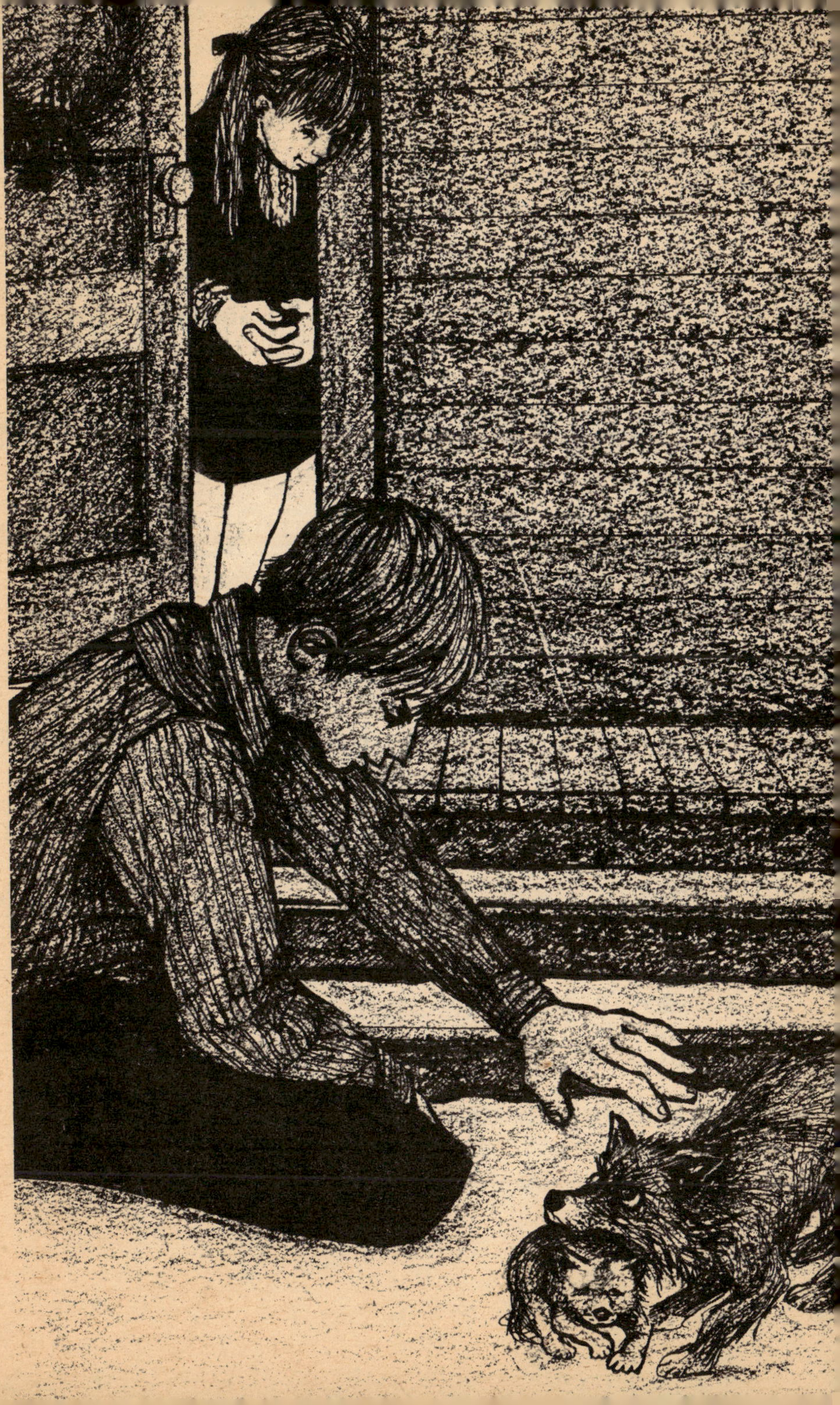

up. "Shall I bring them in, Dad? The puppy doesn't look very healthy."

Mr. Martin paused thoughtfully. "I don't think you'd better, Lon. The dog wouldn't come in and it's not fair to separate them after what she went through to get him here. See if you can get her to follow you to the barn. Beth and I'll get some food and blankets and follow you out. Watch the lights; too much civilization all at once might scare her off."

Lon stuffed the puppy under his shirt and shivered harder when he felt the cold body against his skin. The puppy responded to the warmth and wiggled into a comfortable position. Lon showed Kit that the puppy was safe in his shirt, then he started toward the barn. Kit followed, watching the bulge in his shirt anxiously.

Lon slid the door open and the warmth of

the barn steamed out into the cold air. He felt for the light switch and turned on one dim light at the back of the barn. The cows mooed softly as Lon stepped into the barn. After a moment's hesitation, Kit slipped in after him. Lon carried the puppy to an empty box stall and set it down on a pile of hay.

Soon Mr. Martin and Beth entered the barn carrying blankets and a bowl of milk. Beth had the rest of the roast from dinner, too. Kit seemed at ease so Mr. Martin turned on another light and lifted the puppy. While Lon and Beth fed Kit, he looked at the puppy's leg. It was cut and bruised but the bone wasn't broken. He opened the medicine chest over the feed bins and put a mild disinfectant on the wound, then he put the puppy on a blanket beside Kit.

Kit licked the puppy and looked up at the Martins gratefully. Her tail thumped the hay on the floor of the stall. Lon turned to his father. "Why did you say she wouldn't go in the house, Dad? I bet she would have followed me in."

Mr. Martin steered the children out of the stall and turned off the light. "I hate to disillusion you, but she wouldn't have. She isn't ready for that yet. Sometime maybe. Here she'll be quiet and with the only thing she knows, other animals. She trusts us though and I suspect before spring, she'll be just another member of the family. Let her take her time. I've seldom heard of a dog only having one puppy and that one was hurt so I can pretty well imagine what must have happened out there in the woods. Time and patience, that's what it takes." He closed the barn doors and they walked in silence across the yard.

Inside the house, the children stood in the

living-room window and watched the colored lights twinkle off the snow. Lon looked up at the sky. It was starting to snow. He turned to Beth and grinned. "This is going to be a great Christmas! I even got the dog I wanted."

Beth watched the heavy flakes of snow drift lazily past the reflection of colored light and smiled to herself. After all, there were two dogs.

In the barn, the cows placidly chewed their cuds. Occasionally a stanchion creaked or a mouse scurried across the floor of the hay-mow but there was no other sound. Kit lay with her body curled around the puppy, lost in a deep, peaceful sleep.